Leyton Underground

Michael Clements

PublishAmerica
Baltimore

Softcover 9781462699919
PUBLISHED BY PUBLISHAMERICA, LLLP
www.publishamerica.com
Baltimore

Printed in the United States of America

Leyton Underground
by Michael Clements

This book is dedicated to Dr Verma Hariharan,
an excellent physician

(cover design and b/w images by the author)

Table of Contents

.

LEYTON UNDERGROUND
By Michael Clements

Cheatmeat Soft Soap
Sleepy weepy whores of Harlowe
eat apples on the Night of Fires in the fundamentalist
Temple of the Owl - and all the drunken brawlers,
and sunken kerb crawlers are excluded without hope
from the female cuddle puddle.
Try the soft soap hard grope
after the manly soccer match
and the fool tool stain chain
preferred by cheatmeat pullers
on that night of the furious fires,
when whore haulers hide with the foxes,
when no payment is deferred,
and Beltane, the fresh Gender Blender,
emerges from the blazing logs
and compels with new enchantments
unbelievers to share the sties
and kennels of impotent hogs and three-legged dogs.

Hokki Koki

On the Day of the Dead, the Dagenham Girl Pipers
rise up in clapper-rapping razzle dazzle around
Chingford Mount, and buxom Buckhurst Hill harpies
in white ankle socks make an apocalyptic sound
with their tambourines and paper combs :
the Sea Cadets in their watery graves rise to their knees
and startled crabs crawl out of eye-socket homes
while turbaned mothers seek the best fish dish from the corner
slop shop
to put on the offering table. Dining with the Dead entails
a best clothes pose with the father, and at least
some body-stocking rocking for the teen-age daughter in
disposable clothes.
Every family has a mummy or two in dusty bandages,
a neglected granny, or perhaps her pampered cat,
which they take down from the dresser top,
sanctified by Petosiris as a once-a-year devotional prop,
but nobody really believes in resurrection and all that,
for all their fox-trots and tango strutting and high-stepping,
as none can conceive a next world better than Epping.

Shaggy Doggy is our Bogeyman

Chaos and impenetrable darkness, lit by flashes of occasional
lightning,
cover the skies of Windsor, while idle dreamers in suits of
cloth-of-gold
play cards for kisses with politicians, and order lashes
for the poor and homeless, the ugly and the old.
Now we need our Bogeyman to strike up the Hymn of Freedom
on flute and drum, to strike that chord of defiance
which makes the blood of bankers run cold!
Do not spew when, in his best clothes pose, the Tory lord
rises to his feet and advises the assembled dogsbodies to look
for comfort
in the old black box where the strap-ons are stored.
(It's a well-known fact fake willies are flourished
when budgets are debated in the hallowed Upper House.
For Lord Elgin brought back an antique box from Athens
which the Pasha swore dated to the times of saucy Aristophanes,
and in this box were wooden replacement phalli
which he donated to those feeble nobles who still adorn the
red leather benches.
But I digress, for grander by far than the dildoes of yesteryear
is the mighty broomstick of Alice of Dunmow, mistress of
Henry II,
which the Lionheart carved into an object of fealty and feudal
duty,
a phallus pointing from the jaws of a Plantagenet leopard,
and which has since been shoved up the arses of ministers
prime,
those middle class poodles raised up from the common slime,

as they knelt in humility to swear their sacred oath of loyalty
to the monarch.
O Yes! In England, that escalator for transporting the lower
up into the upper middle class, all need to learn the arts of
grovelling
before greed and power based on birth. So let the poor lose all
they have
to feed the unaccountable mirth of their betters, for it's always
been the way
to deny the Shaggy Doggy called Fenris his bowl of lights,
only making his hunger more strong, his shadow longer by
day,
and his vengeance more certain through the coming nights.

Summer Waters Still

Willow hangs over the pool,
leaves drift past, slowly, in circles,
only a water-boatman, hopping on the stream
questions this spell of torpor.
Sighing, yawning, half in dream,
the girl peers down from the branch
hoping to glimpse her future lover's face
among the ripples, by the felled and mossy tree.
She sees only the ducks competing for pride of place,
and her feline quest, alas!, does not include me.

Touch and Distance Healing

The wet-nurse of the sacred flame hums holy cantos
by the camp-fire, and the people rest nodding
half asleep while Mother Wolf suckles her cubs :
this is the time when the Spirit of Flame arises
from the embers and dancing strikes a pose
with arms outstretched - no plodding
earthly music in these lightning flashes
but cascading symphonies of inter-galactic flares !
These days, rainbows can be used for etheric travel.
62 light years distant, Zuben Elgenubi, dispenses
Caesar's justice, the claws of the Scorpion cut off
by senatorial decree to form calm Libra, and you can unravel
too like bold Julius the threads spun by the Fates,
and expose heaven to the common gaze !
Nod to the good vibrations, as they burst apart the gates
of that burning ground of all future tenses,
and let the druid draw forth music from the standing stone
with a fiddle bow, and dance on the Scales of Life and Death!
Dancing on burning embers by the light of a crescent moon
Flame can move the shadows with small gestures,
and that fellow with a cast in one eye will run to hide
behind a rock from the witch and the summoned Fates~
in vain, of course ! In a distant field of meadowsweet
the Scarecrow - that First Scarecrow who has always been
since the beginning the guardian of the first sown field of
wheat~
is struck by lightning and burns beneath the bright cloud tide.
I advise you to fill your pockets with cemetery earth,
when the season of storms emerges from the green hills

and the wires snap and jerk on the telegraph poles,
and, placing your hands on the ancient standing stone,
to pray in this way : " O Great Mother, give birth !"

Meditation outside the Moghkadeh

The poor, tired old fiend coughs up coins
like a lucky slot machine,
while the wind from the Sahara
carries warm whispers and sand
from distant, mysterious Tatouine.
A huge silver half crown rolls into my hand
like a miniature Wheel of Ixion,
and the Devil's daughter grins
as she paints her toe-nails green.
I, who have lampooned the clowns,
jugglers, contortionists and collaborators
of Westminster, must now tell stories in the dust
of a foreign place to earn a kindly crust.
I'll not take coppers for my tales,
ha'pennies and sticky farthings,
but only shillings, silver marks,
even the five franc gilded fraud of the third
Napoleon, any coin which won't shame the scales,
even if it bear the double-headed bird
of a shameful Czar, or the seal of the Sultan.
Release now the tormented souls from the bitumen
for they only took a wrong turning in Becontree
and fell through the cracks in the pavement,
don't you see, O Master of the Dual Mystery
I've sand beneath my finger-nails, but I haven't stirred
from the Bokhara rug in my bedroom, even when I heard
a phone ringing with news from nowhere, Tartary
(or boring Bangalore) about an offer of repentance
rewarded by the Apostate Bishop of Basildon.

Just take *that* bastard's soul as payment down instead!
I'll add a few black stones from the River Gandakee,
and then we can all applaud Satan for setting the innocent free.

Slimming Haiku

My belly pokes out
shyly, like a contented,
adulterous wife.

Dog Tanka

"I can spot a shapely bum from thirty feet,"
I said to Shaggy Doggy with a smile.
He grinned: "But I can smell one
from a quarter of a mile."

Runaway

There was a dead man in a car outside the library,
his face expressionless, as though expecting death
to be but a continuation of non-events.
I was raised by wolves and am a son of magic.
To escape the demons which hover in cruel suspense,
I avoid straight lines and travel in circles instead.
I am forced to wear the clothes of the dead
and I must eat the food rejected by others.
I look a little marginalised because of it.
But my free existence has never been tragic:
I'm no idle dreamer, and have sucked at the grey wolf's tit
with my hairy brothers and sisters.
You may wear boots of alligator hide, and flash a wallet
filled with dubious currency, but your feet will still get blisters,
and the demons cannot be bought off, I fear.
Better to run and fight on, forgetting smug acceptance.
Slip between light and darkness like Brother Wolf,
for resistance is the headiest drug of all, my dear.

Thrice-Great

Hermes is a whizz-kid,
and never takes the fall-
an Aquarian by instinct
he can ride a celestial skid,
by acting all mercurial.

The Infernal Theme-Park holds Games

Follow the treasure trail on the electrified rail
with ears burning and feet a-smoking,
with the toadies and creepers and lowly floppers,
all wannabe night-club bee-boppers
mingling with West End shoppers,
and Brixton sloppers, a haggle-drazzle
of whipper-snappers who long to be rappers,
in a rain-soaked kaleidoscope
which all deserves preservation,
as a sanitised middle-class prat reservation.

You need only a deacon to decorate,
when it comes to window design whores,
but a purple-frocked bishop to desecrate
the lingerie range in the best department stores.

"Sing Hosiery in the highest!" will be the watchword,
for streetwalkers look nuder in crotchless knickers
when Babalon squats once more on Her scarlet throne.
(True-believers will wave fake disabled driver stickers
as parking will be strictly controlled in the Erogenous Zone.)

The sleepwalkers of Leyton come back to walk their old
haunts,
blown into a broken concrete scree by an explosive council
decree.
Their mischievous certainty may be heard after midnight in
taunts
hurled at the asylum-seeking sleepers on damaged beds
bought cheaply from the secondhand benefactor of bug and
flea,
but they cannot clearly find their way by dismal foggy day,

'cause all has been transmogrified by official spittle on the map display.

The Fairy of the Leather Laces will trip you up if you run away without even attempting to pay, so take care my sleepy-heads. and utter a little prayer to Hermes, the Whizz Kid, King of Thieves, to wake up still normal, securely tucked up in your normal beds.

Stronghold of Infamy

From the year dot
through ages of famine
they've boiled their own pot
and fed the Procession Grand
of dwarves, jugglers and clowns
which serves their interest
throughout the gloomy land.
The devil in blue guards the Gothic gate
and grins like a bastard's brat
when he salutes with palm outspread
but all ignore his Hand of Fate.
Many of these top-hatted fools fold
like cardboard dollies and play dead
when the divisions are called
because poverty is unelectable
and their butter knows
the right side of bread.

Exalted Music

Playing the standing stone with a violin bow
music becomes slumber and song is a dream
when the choir of wolves make all forget pain ;
the satyr wears a silk top hat and dances slow
on the stepping blocks across the stream
and the schoolgirl looks back again
into the inviting darkness and sunset glow.
O Orpheus! Do not let her go, for all the world
needs the new sown wheat to grow,
and hungers for a lamp to lead the dancers on :
life which holds death back :
the brilliant soul in the lightless black.

Rubber Stones

In the beginning rocks were alive and split
to make more rocks : our ancestors got sick
of jumping out of the way of rocks on a spree
and being kept awake by rocks making love noisily.
So they put a curse of fatal freezing on them all
which took away their petreous wit,
and cast them into an earthy pit
of immovability - a dirty trick !
Thus we apes, the snout-lechers and shout-fetchers
inherited the cosmos as gigglers and higglers,
pluggers and muggers, barons and Sharons,
we, the treasure-seekers and pleasure-wreakers,
with our lost poodle eyes sneaked on to the stage
like washing-line knicker-thieves in dirty sneakers
and rubber pants bodyline chafers to rant and rage
against our pitiful mortality, we poor open-fly
peepers and tumescent itchers became
bend-over bullies with sad little willies, who sigh,
feeling as out of place as a mucky pup in a palace cup -
all because tight frocks invite bum shocks
and Rag Week is really Shag Week and fisting
unites dumbfucks with bum fucks which we hate !
And all the rocks can do now is to wait and wait and wait....

Zulmat

Remember to leave your shoes
at the door of instruction in the dark
lest you step on the teacher's lesson-plan
and leave a dirty mark.

Iron Sex Slackers

In the wishy-washy world of media whoosh tubes
slide the Empty Suits of plonker pillock harm,
all baby-blue waddlers and bum paddlers
who like to drag you into the TV bath
but prove underwater climax bunglers.
Young newshounds must remain calm
when urged to employ velvet brocade festoonments
to their innocent fundaments and cry :
"Chaos ! Chaos! Stop Thief !"and (with contempt) reject
the Clever Order of the Royal Dung Beetle as a total lie.

From the superglued legoland of the BBC
step the shapeshifters and the shitlifters
palms outretched for alms in return for fake veracity:
clanking and spanking, the shitheelers and faith-healers.
the shape- shifters and skirt-lifters do a little dance
on overhead wires, for this is the Avenue of Blancmange Pie
where you spend a lot for sweets which do not satisfy.

Inevitable Acts of Magic

Defamed, debauched, debagged and destroyed
whisps of cindery trouserhood, their blackened bones
smoke like nutty slack coke still chained to the stake
stuck in the courtyard of a Westminster palace:
the perished heirs of the Welsh Wizard torn from their thrones,
the shitkickers and snotflickers, blackberrypickers
and yoghurt lidlickers, models in wet T-shirts and blue
knickers,
a whole tribe of Liberal lords and Democrat crones
sent packing by rebels in schools run by fools,
by boys trampled by police horses
brought in from surrounding forces.
So, when a bit of a thug with an ugly mug,
and his blue-coated creatures with horrible features
start killing the Children of the Revolution,
look for the Wall-Eyed Vulture in the sky
dropping his shit whilst decrying pollution,
and turn up the sweat-box music
which translates whipper-snappers into cap-busting rappers,
and get ready to boogie.
Don't believe the banks are good for you,
or that the Members of the House are anatomically correct
when the big blown up dollies and big blow-out bellies
connect.

The Lost Limpidity of my Waking Words

Like a sickening cello solo the beggar in ermine
whines outside their Lordships' silver mine,
this donkey of our ruling class posing before an open door
from which Liberal Democrats *en masse*
pour to piss upon the children of the poor.
A cobbler, a hobbler, a whopper apple-bobber,
all take the social democrat ticket with knock-kneed drearies,
fairy cake philosophers, horse doctors playing the fool,
stuttering fly-fishermen on the sly living in high eyries
on the Isles of Mars, all become Treasury sneeries;
-and only a grease-monkey from Hartlepool
with a two foot wrench could rearrange
their precedences in the State Opening of Gobbing
when our masters congratulate each other's robbing.

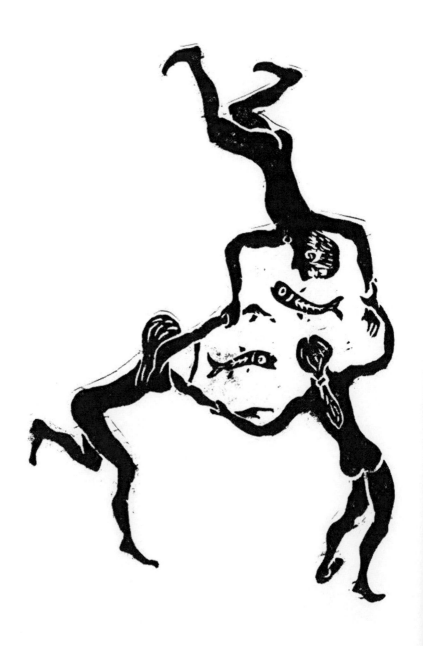

Corsets of Brass

The witchfinder is senile, a duff dud
debased by sparkling drugs who cottages
for kicks: better write poetry underwater
than take his sodden advice,
for there is no protection in the mud
from one step and the next
when Varoucha Gargolis acts all nice
and invites you in to sin.
Just avoid her little house in the forest
and as for sad old Selim Yusuf, the Son of Sin,
the smeller-out of the unclean,
I last saw him lashed to an A-frame
on a flat-bed truck driven by the Rubbish Police,
screaming for mercy whilst being flogged
for dumping human waste in his wheelie-bin.

Buddhist Haiku

I've been to Heaven
and the only thing I saw there
was a looking glass.

City of Philosophers

Spandrils and cornices, columns and classical
architraves with corybantes in the angles,
smirking lapiths groping statuary
clad in flesh-tinted tights covered in spangles:
the Grand Parade of the Feel and Fondle Police
led by Paul of Edelweiss the gorilla killer-
he pays five hundred euros for an *orang utan* skull
being a determined creationist.
(His wife, the Infanta of Aragon,
is no domestic paragon
and sells her husband's secrets to the Pentagon.)
And outside the city walls, where life is dull
lurk bare in the woods crappers,
mad-cap flappers chased by aging rappers,
with Ordnance Survey mappers
running behind like the clappers,
all in flesh imitating the public art
made exemplary (but remote and lost)
by their wise and solemn masters within.
Do you know a City like this ?
If so, mark it on the Almagest of Hell
as one to be avoided at any cost.

Gobsmack Smiles

The skank man has drowned in plonk,
his mountain bike buried with him
in Coronation Gardens : he had the flow
of piggy sniggering schoolgirls from Wanstead
who went giggly at the sight of his wonder willy-
all despite simper Sunday in the suburbs
when the daddies' slippers *thwang* !
Among the happy doss-house mollies
see the bright and dazed-eyed dollies
skedaddle like termites caught in syrup
from the doodle-danglers and their master's fun-boodle;
there will be baseball bat whacks
for competing bootblacks and testicle-shaving
for all who're craving baby-oil
under glitter-balls when motor-cycles thunder
into the Zen of an ever-expanding seminal coil.

Inflatable Brides

(after Martial)
It 's not enough to let some bum-fluff yobbo
play the *junglee* Boy Wolf and hang around
your little girl like some superfly hound:
when I was young I fell under the spell of such a crush
despite my love of ascetic self-control
and began to use sandalwood soap like a dope,
and those memories still patrol
my sensitivities and make me blush.
Eat black pudding and horse radish in a bucket,
stuff gunny-sacks of tripe and onions in your belly:
wash in horse-piss and steal your clothes
from ruined scarecrows and some down-and-out jack-
and the pungent odour of excited youth
may be hidden by another more uncouth,
thus keeping the avid harpies off your track

The Wall-eyed Vulture

I see the circling ministerial vulture
and his chinless turkey-buzzard pals
looking for fresh victims to pick clean:
for the global gloat in his throat
keeps the City afloat,
and all those aristo shits
in white shirt fronts
follow his lead
in the Mansion House *splitz*.

Australia Haiku

Railways and roads grow
across those hot, endless plains
like squiggling varicose veins.

Spindleshanks wears a Top Hat

The hand-job of a teasing Tom limits
the cider stupor of layabouts and condemns
to oblivion worries about the political loyalties
of blatherskites and nutty slack interlopers
in that great whorehouse by the yellow Thames.
Still he strides down the corridors of his finite mind
all over the back benches like a fifteen shilling shoddy suit
with human skin patches on the elbows and knees:
he is the Saviour of the Ruling Class, his very own kind,
collecting the tears of Moss Side and the blood of Bradford
to cool the rick-rack-rackety turntable
upon which Westminster is built: concrete ramps
and metal bars keeping out the voters
because nobody plays "The Red Flag" on a barrel-organ
or believes in freedom any more except the tramps,
lying like grey scatter cushions around every War Memorial:
no idle dreamer, but a bogey of the Third Order,
a cloth-of-gold con-man born to a banker and a disappointed
Gorgon.

Pinned Cockroaches

The Death Universe is littered
with the shells of snails and other
hermaphrodites : many Blairs float in glue
unable to return here and others, much embittered
by the unsatisfying nature of positive
self-glorification, stink up the place
like so many Thatchers in aspic.
Here, in the Life Universe,
crazy kids break crazy codes
to get at crazy downloads
and find a new rationale in public disgrace
when overindulgence makes them sick:-
for you can be a revolutionary slacker
and shock the world by doing nothing-
this is the hardcore truth:
your parents want you to fail
just like them. If you try to change *this* universe,
they'll call the cops on you and tell a tale.

The Heartbeat of the Universe

The fire-eaters and sleight-of-hand mavericks,
and the sellers of dead batteries all play tricks
with visitors in this Hall of Distorting Mirrors:
these lovers of an abominable joke
giggle and splutter and give your ribs a poke
when you gasp and tremble during their audition
as fixer of our boo-boo dreams. Their glad-handing
at the funerals of stars is as shocking
as to see a fresh corpse in a body-stocking
go clapper-rapping and razzle-dazzle in the morgue.
Don't encourage the Discombobulator of Perdition
in his unnatural pursuits - leave that to the bishops in blue
on the Day of the Dead to do.
In Orion Betelgueuse is now a fading superstar,
but promises to explode on his celestial commode,
and change that constellation beyond recognition,
which is sad for those who like things as they are.

The Secret Smile Scam of a Political Leonardo

Full of munch and mutter, a crowd-pulling
media circus sensation, this bloody-fingered
shit-slinger from the Back of Beyond offers
the Princes of the East his contraptions
for crowd-culling, the clankety-banging rattle-tattle
of civilian death, propelled by the dirty laughter
of an errant wizard : this is the log in the water
that rips off the leg of your daughter;
this is the man with the horsehair brushes
who'll paint you a red mural for your last supper;
this is the mapper and sapper come to rough up your foe,
flattering you up till you can't say no-
so join the penitential shuffle of the shifty suppliiers
and buy British guns and ammunition,
join up the dots and complete the enigmatic fresco.

The Coal Code

Write it in nutty slack before the teacher comes back,
write it on your school heroes' plaque,
that the trousers of the world are falling down
and our rulers have got hairs stuck in their crack.
They say that in the Buddhist Hell the demons
have rubber-tipped pitchforks and tickle
the damned 'till they repent -or (in the worst cases)
give them Chinese burns or French kisses with a chilli pickle,
and this is true, but not for much longer,
as the devils are on the march and getting stronger.
Sick of stereotypical marginalisation as prison guards,
they demand retraining as care workers
and better prospects for promotion up the scale
to supervisory roles : Hell is going to pot for sure,
now that the Catholic one has been shut down for keeps,
and when our masters finally die it'll be nothing more
than a holiday camp for Blairs, Thatchers and other creeps.

A Day of Fire and Diamonds

I read the Book of Transmigration
in a spired Gothic railway station
while waiting for the train to Hell :
but cannot find a suitable spell.
I ignore the cash and Carey
Christian, begging for the cause.
but have to close the tedious tome,
and stare blankly up at the Byzantine dome :
money-mongering by grinny people
hits the ear like a cracked bell in the Anglican steeple,
and the sermons of the oppressors jar the gut
like yesterday's supper, petrified and stale fish-fried.
I rise and walk the damp corner where the glugger bugger
died,
not wanting to buy crude food from a rude dude
I have to move on past the Albanians
engaged in intimate retailing, but unable to compete
with the velvet mousetraps
under the skirts of dissident
housewives on awayday benders
promising black waspies and silver bootstraps
in return for new dishwashers and shining blenders.
I avoid the weekenders, flying the flag in drag,
the teasers with plastic tweezers, all future Blairs
slithery eels with shifty deals for the Holy Father of Greed,
Murdoch the new national grinning diabolus.
And so, maybe I'll take the bus instead
and sit next to a Man of Dread
praising the virtues of liberated weed
exalted in the Choir of Hosts
and with a shrug, join in the chorus.

The River Roding Bypasses Chigwell

It's a panoramic porno picture from the air,
full of palaces with swimming-pools
where gardens are blurred by smoking barbecues
and housewives in sunglasses sprawl on the grass bare.
Here nymphs kick off their high-heeled shoes
and run around in packs, tossing the pie-crust
of their youth into the bent hedgerows,
rolling shrieking younger brothers in the dust,
and rubbing their ponies' horseshit into the little boys' hair,
to their the lifestyle trainer's delight and mother's despair.

This is paradise where the White Van Men prosper
and stuff green figs and ice-cream into gaping mouths,
whilst their bankers plot to pull down windmills
and spread car-parks over the unproductive hills:
the land of bangle-janglers in recycled Wranglers
dangling newfangled i-phones from tattooed wrists,
bouncing babies and bouncing breasts
all gathered under the St George's Cross
but ignorant of the changing times of profit and loss,
because the forest plans to flourish anew
and see the road to Basildon choked by vines.
A hedge of briars will cut off the cavorters,
the boob-jobbed mothers and gold-toothed daughters,
the fat rich bastards with Alfa-Romeos
who dole out loans at enormous rates,
and all will fall into a morbid doze
without hope of resurrection by a passing creep,
masquerading as a kissable prince
dancing the Essex night away with pockets deep -
for there will be no awakening for the suburban slut,
no private wedding followed by public divorce

as the reward for marrying up and up.

The despoilers and wasters will face a fate which amazes,
beneath the chains of dandelions and uncultivated daisies:
chaos and impenetrable darkness, lit by flashes
of occasional lightning, will cover the skies of Ilford,
while idle dreamers in suits of cloth-of-gold
play cards for kisses with politicians, and order lashes
for the riotous poor, the ugly and the old.

Now we need the Bogeyman to strike up the Hymn
of Freedom on flute and drum, to strike that chord
of defiance which makes the blood of bankers run cold,
and sets sky-dancing the magpies with intelligent eyes
and animates scarecrows to join the throng
with "Ca Ira! " as their revolutionary song.

High Jive Jinx on the High Street

I love the twilight when things are more than they seem,
for the phantoms become gold from brassy drottle,
and the apes which stumble in the jungle
straighten up and join in the urban rush-hour bungle :
and the skipper of a garbage-scow can see
through the distorting lens of his raised vodka bottle
a whole new Arcadia across the estuary.
This is no flare of inconsequential despair
from the solar. furnace but a visionary burst
from lab-al-lahoot which impacts below :
better to drink cardamom tea to the beat
in the house than fight in the lavatory
with the dragon and the horse
to muffled saxaphones playing in your head : treat
all dealers to a kiss when the pills pop.
"Don't stop !" they whine : "Don't stop !"

But have you heard the visionary word ?
The Great Beast has left the building
and gone east to look for repossession claims,
and where he passes the economy is in flames.
Follow His treasure trail on the electrified rail
with ears burning and feet a-smoking,
with the toadies and creepers and lowly floppers,
all wannabe night-club bee-boppers
mingling with West End shoppers,
and Brixton sloppers, a haggle-drazzle
of whipper-snappers who long to be rappers,
in a rain-soaked kaleidoscope
which all deserves no preservation,
as a sanitised middle-class prat reservation
but needs the torch of a funeral pyre consecration.

You need only a deacon to decorate,
when it comes to window design whores,
but a purple-frocked bishop to desecrate
the lingerie range in the best department stores.

"Sing Hosiery in the highest !"will be the watchword,
for streetwalkers look nuder in crotchless knickers
when Babalon squats once more on Her scarlet throne.
(True-believers will wave fake disabled driver stickers
as parking will be strictly controlled in the Erogenous Zone.)

The sleepwalkers of Leyton come back to walk their old
haunts,
blown into a broken concrete scree by an explosive council
decree.
Their mischievous certainty may be heard after midnight in
taunts
hurled at the asylum-seeking sleepers on damaged beds
bought cheaply from the secondhand benefactor of bug and
flea,
but they cannot clearly find their way by dismal foggy day,
'cause all has been transmogrified by official spittle on the
map display.

The Fairy of the Leather Laces will trip you up if you run
away
without even attempting to pay, so take care my sleepy-heads.
and utter a little prayer to Hermes, the Whizz Kid, King of
Thieves,
to wake up still normal, securely tucked up in your normal
beds.

A Simoon from the South

A simoon from the south claws at blinded Essex
with fingers of Libyan sand and all the Grand Army of Hell
rides behind with dusty banners and rusty truncheons...
Number not the fallen angels, when the town council
invites the Beast to walk the street and do not stand aside
like the balloon bursters and blink firsters,
the Basildon snot-gobblers and cock-wobblers
first in buggery and thuggery behind a closed door,
but file out to protect what is right and comely
in this everlasting and unreasoning war.
Don't listen to the foot-draggers and sheep-shaggers,
the husband-naggers and tongue-waggers who look daggers
at girls in headscarves on the streets of Braintree.
Let's turn the mountains upside down upon our masters,
and illuminate the secret face of the night
with ancient truths of liberty and equality,
make chaotic the smug calculations of investors,
for the only choice we have is to be free !

Thrifty Haiku

Needing new curtains
I pasted yesterday's *Sun*
on to the blank panes.

Men in Masks

The penitential shuffle of the shifty candidates
sometimes gets us down and we want to slap them around -
a bit-
rough them up for lying and thieving from us voters,
or transform them into bloated floaters
by a beam-heavy dream levee
at the mouth of the Orinoco : (I should *koko)*
but we never act like a head-banger
reindeer-whanger from Stavanger
or the rough sleepers with red peepers
who hurl beer cans at the fox-hunt leapers
(haw-haw-haw)
or the wine-drinkers and ethyline weepers,
the fakers and Quakers, DT shakers and pop-pill bakers
who never vote at all...
There's no shame for grannies on the game
who can earn everlasting fame
by servicing (with a whip) Lord Haw-Haw of Snore-Snore
and spilling all to *Blick* or *Paris Match*
because another shifty lord owns all the gutter press
in the Land of Nutty Slack and can do no less
than oblige his fellow nobles like a true parliamentary whore.

Rattletrap Dustcart Wars

It rankles a VIP to have his trousers around his ankles
in zones where you can't hide from drones,
dumping their loads like dustbinmen
who can't count to ten
but know when it's safe to zoom off again.
It can give anyone abdominal gripes,
that distant sound of victorious bagpipes,
beckoning on the under-tippers
and political day-trippers
to cavort with the booters and shooters
while their tour-guide flakes out and lies
in an empty beer barrel like a dead Diogenes
nourished by explosive Van Gogh skies.
The electorate is supposed to be admiring
of all that purposeful perspiring,
that flying the flag in drag
like Achilles in a sister's dress
and to forget the wearisome mess
that death brings on bright-burning wings.

Cutting the Product with Snot, or Not

Swag men and bag men reverence
that savage sailor with a holed shag bag
who has been to distant climes
(many times)
through choppy seas and driving rain,
and as I limp after him through dark gateways
I too expect the devil at the door to salute
even if I'll never return to that point again.
I must stumble on, looking for his tracks,
-the weeping women are a trusty guide-
for this path to Hades is quite littered
with discarded condoms and dead wild men :
eventually I'll catch up to my erstwhile shipmate
and try not to act embittered
at being left behind to a prosaic fate :
"Tell me," I'll demand, " a new tale which Homer left out."
His teeth will flash white in the dim light,
and even now I know his reply will be :
"To alter one part of the fabric will undo the rest,
so be content, shipmate, with *this* reality."

In the Land of Nutty Slack

Drink deep of the Goat
and make your laughter loud and dirty
when that log in the water
drags off your daughter
and no errant wizard will brave the brown stream :
roll over and smile at your betters
for resistance only leads to dismay
and the bloated bluecoats
will put the boot in your dream.
Leave the percolated old farts
to decorate with flags their tiny handcarts
for their faith is an inner asphyxiation,
their allegiance is to rotting flesh,
the stench of dead children
and sm0king mosques in Qandahar.
The privileged always believe in themselves,
and wish only for an unchanging shoreline :
but the future is an unforgiving wave
for those who can't behave,
and the wing-beats of Nemesis are no longer far.

Buy Edward Lear a Beer

We export more flesh than any other country
for a nation of our size,
which is why we punch above our weight,
the Lonsdale Belt above our hairy arse
though it means a flattened bottom-
but who cares about the underclass ?
Write it in jail code
on the infant school plaque,
that they may learn by heart :
"I am poor, wretched and unlearned,
no loss at all when you send me away
to die from a bomb planted by dusty road."
We never get to rough up our masters,
roll them around in the gents' lav,
stick shit down their lying throats,
because they're well-protected
in garden suburbs by huge gates and moats.
They all abhor violence, loving the peace
of glad hands clasped over a fresh grave,
which doesn't contain a child of their own, of course,
and all they fear is the one generation
that will at last not learn to behave.

King Toot of Tooting

King Toot of Tooting has gone down shooting,
and his men have done some looting
in the lock-up of Mr Big Shot, that unseemly blot,
who sells guns to swag men and bag men,
bad-breathed pimps, Albanian gimps and shag-hag wimps.
Here the royal *ushabti* can all tool up like feisty knaves,
slapping each other's knee
and giggling with anticipatory glee.
But first they'll lay their master to rest
beside his parents' weed-grown graves,
then, still in their black suits of sorrow,
down tumblers of Cuban rum at the wake,
as though there's no tomorrow,
finally filing out the door
to don rubber masks and settle the ongoing score.
King Toot slumbers on in his funeral gear,
his spark of life winking no more,
draped like his ancestors with amulets,
a lot of gold and lying texts about an afterlife,
and all he can say to the Crocodile God is :
"False testimony ! Hell, no !
I always kept my fingers crossed when I swore !"

Kali is a Smasher !

I was raised by wolves in the greenwood,
my infant eye squinting up at Polaris,
and I saw long shadows in the landscape
cast by wild men in chariots
tearing back the dawn :
the r5ed-faced demon defiled the stellar nursery,
tearing out the bottle green shards
of frozen ammonia with his claws
and still threatens limb-chopping
and deep-veined cruelties to this day.
But Mother Wolf will save mankind
for the unnumbered time
and get a pat from the Black Goddess,
and we'll all dance a measure
on the burning ground
with Shaggy Doggy
and his kindred rescued from the pound.

Bird Men of Alexandria

Long shadows beneath the Pharos
as the evening light is lit
to acknowledge the blue, red and gold sky :
Hipparchus is off to a state dinner at the palace,
optimistic and without a care,
his grey head full of bright ideas,
while the tired traders pack up their stalls
and public slaves sweep out the market square.
Tonight the philosophers will argue about
flight and rising to the stars like gods.
(Ptolemy is interested in the military aspects.)
And a traveller from a distant land will but in:
"In China they have hot air balloons
and great kites which can carry a man aloft !"
Ptolemy frowns : "But what's to prevent
unsavoury commoners from flying
over the palace and spying on the royal women
as they bathe in the blue lotus swimming pool ?"
Ptolemy glares : "Do you take me for a fool ?
There's a hint of Athenian democracy
in this idea !" The philosophers show some hesitation,
and librarian Apollonius changes the subject:
"I've been thinking about a printing press,
which will be a boon to education,
and mean that every man can own a book."
The traveller broke in : "In China they make
this paper from rags and print thousands of volumes
very cheaply." "Hrumpf !" says Ptolemy.
When young Heron tries to broach the financing

of his steam engine, which can move tons
of rocks from quarries, Ptolemy asks, icily,
"What are we going to do with all the unemployed
quarrymen ? Teach them to read books
about revolution ?" The king dismisses
the scientists, sneering :" Gentlemen, you are like
the birds in that play by Aristophanes
who create a feathered parliament
and then make a great deal of noise, achieving nothing !"
They are waved away without the customary gifts,
missing the flute girls and the fire breathers,
the Nubian dancers in ostrich feathers,
not even receiving a blue lotus posey,
and then have to wait outside the shut gates
for a public taxi. But here, Eratosthenes the geographer
has a word with the traveller and goes home in haste
to produce revised illustrated maps of the world,
showing China and a scrambled India :
so the evening is not an entire waste.

Surprise Haiku

Surprised schoolgirl look,
Japanese face screws up
a Cockney accent.

Hiccup Haiku

Lost drunken girls
are scattered across the town
like wet pearls for swine.

Sexually Explicit Haiku

Granny's on the game,
life will never be the same-
teen-age sex to blame.

God's Xmas Message

In many ways I'm
almost human , but know that
I am that I am..

The Snake is his Umbilical Cord

He squats in the Palace of Westminster
like a malevolent toad just across the road...
and his prowler flunkies, like demented howler monkeys,
hunt down head-bangers who drop clangers
in tracts of shame filled with NAME upon NAME
and mangle the press stranglers with brief-cases in hangars,
and give them a sorry soaking in shit (and no joking)
just to protect the chinless wonders from historical blunders,
to safeguard the knicker-knackers and titled wisecrackers
who misbehave with flattering loons under mind-shattering
moons
alongside scatty, batty schoolgirls with natty fake pearls,
those heroes and Neros who dog the poolside jumper
and schoolride thumper on the lookout for something
plumper....
He squats in his gated community of fat-arsed ladies and lords
all drooling etiquette for the parliamentary frauds
and nobody notices the stench because they've filled in the
trench,
paid off the cops with crowns on their hats all righty,
and his deputy's happy to see him so high and mighty...

The Salamander

Burn the LCD TV in the window, and take a gander
at the glowing scales of the salamander
and his ruby red eyes touched with a flare
of otherworld weariness and jaded despair.
We are gold, not dross, and may appear to stumble
in the jungle, but that's a mere illusion
flickering on the walls of our caves,
as we are more than the chaos outside
the inner sanctum of our being.
Take a tip from the rough sleepers with red peepers,
the subterranean creepers, the ethyline weepers,
the Australian wine shakers and the hash brownie bakers,
and when the Tory balloon bursts from inner asphyxiation,
be sure to escape from the burning shop
with your bag of fries and carton of slop,
and leave the financiers to a rapid deflation.
Let those odds and sods, clod with hotrods,
bagmen and fag men, not to mention drag men,
earn burning glances at High School dances,
and sit at High Table with the cold-pressers and cross dressers,
and bark orders to the corpulent flatfeet
pounding a Canary Wharf beat today-
but promised a promotion tomorrow.
Let our wall-eyed Cabinet take their chances
when they go for a romp in the swimmedy swamp,
Let them slap each other on the back,
And make each other very rich, than richer,
because the final reckoning is on the way.

The Cave Artist Haiku

I painted Death there
on my wall : he refuses
to come down again.

A Prayer for the Animation of Buildings

Mother of mysteries liberate poor Merlin
from that dimensionless, lightless and lost oak.
Listen to this plea, that London might yet be free
of Mammon and his monuments, and all those who
grovel at his clay feet : especially bankers.
Look at the map of their City - you will see
a strange pattern emerging of lines, squares,
circles, pentacles and mystic sextiles,
sited on old churches, ancient mounds, graves
and Mithraica. Keep on looking, find
the underlying blueprint : Stock Exchange
to Bank to St Alphage, a right-angled
triangle, enclosing St Margaret
Lothbury, another Wren curio :
and an excellent start for our rough art.
Traffic-flow, you know, is part of it, noise
muffled by narrow streets but directed upward
like puritan hymns in those lightless, grim
churches : but a better effect comes from long
processions on holy days - the ancient
Chaldaeans knew the craft well - and we should
make use of the Shagga Jag Carnival,
and its stone-breaking, pigeon-plummeting,
foundations-flaying, black hole of jittery-jolly
NOISE.
With one grand rattle may their City
tear loose from its steel and concrete stanchions
and float away past Wanstead Flats leaving
a pit abysmal, empty of the diabolical throne.

Then may Bran return home, Lord of Lightful
Things, and make fruitful bowers of these sad,
demonic temples. So might the maidens
make again the mad May dance, toss flowers out of doors
for heroes to catch, and make us forget
false accounting, convenient lies and profitable wars.
Farewell, you sons of bitches, usurers and lackies
of brummagem riches as your square mile goes astray
into the mud of the estuary somewhere near
Gravesend and becomes a clay Pompeii.

Master of the Lightning

You may wake me from sleep,
calling on the cold north wind,
but I do not fear for teeth in the dark
and my shabby pillow of ferns
holds my spirit steady in dream.
Some days I can feast on cheesecake,
and others keep holy by fasting,
and some days can trudge many miles
and others dedicate to meditation.
Many are envious of this pilgrimage,
hating their mired lives,
and curse me when I dance to the slow
music of the Pleiades, but being
a seventh son of Mother Earth,
I am Master of the Lightning
and can read whole histories
in the charred stumps of trees,
and find nuggets of gold
turned up by the thunderbolt.

Immortal

Cast off this shadow and soar :
tell unkind Death that I have left
and am unobtainable, for I ride
dragons astride in the purple evening.
See below, my castle is prepared for me,
the candles are all lit for guests
and my servants have prepared
a solemn banquet. I have drunk
from the cup of Holy Wisdom
and now I can move the lightning
with my shoulder and turn red
pillar-boxes like prayer-wheels.
and drink your rum for Baron Samedi.
There is no double-entry book-keeping
in my dukedom and I have banished
the bogey-men beyond the black stump
and the Great White Stone :
stroll through this art-gallery and museum
of eternity as a tourist, but always
behave with the self-assurance
of a born resident, and smoke your cigar.

The Sons and Daughters of Much the Miller's Son

Washed out, worked up, and wasted well away,
they've not yet learned to fight back and win,
but steal from each other and from us.
They're the revolution which never took place,
and they've mothers who gnawed the face
and ballocks of their fathers, year by sacrificial year.
Everybody fails now except the builders of prisons,
and the makers of jack-boots and police uniforms :
the bombs fall on babies and nursing mothers,
all far away, never fear, but the young know
that the world is sinking, faster and faster,
under that knicker-sniffing, drug-squad snitching middle-age
spread -
as the french-tickler stickler kings of the monkey-troupe
suspect that Marxist waiters spit in their soup,
and hardly bother to steam the stale supermarket bread :
that the chamber-maids are mini-bar moochers,
that the chefs buy in from pooch-stealing takeaways,
stolen retrievers into marinated cutlets,
all hamburger deceivers of financial wizards and fading divas,
and that the prevalent creed of greed, greed, greed
is too bourgeois to succeed, succeed, succeed.
While the rent-boys think that the Right-Honourable Grinbelly
is just another fulminating telly-toff with underpants piss-
smelly,
Babylon is ground into shards by cranks in tanks,
and smirking paedophiles in black plead for children in need.
The poor lose all when their masters run out of petty change;
everything is now interlinked : make a child bleed in Coleraine
and one in burning Fellujah cries out in pain.

Maskara Abullabat

Dance with your little drum,
bells around your ankles,
for we demand an ongoing treat
in the shadow of the Jaggery Mart.
Here the dragon-flow of cosmic juice
creates a nexus in the continuum,
and the currents from Mexico meet
Egyptian mysteries set loose
by ancient prayers which only now start
to move the chambers of green Gaea's heart.
And all the jesters and jokers - that crew
who hang out in the deserted malls at midnight
will be moved to dance the polka out of sight
on greasy chicken bones and evil-smelling spew.
Shitting in shop-doorways is a folk-heritage
which even newcomers try to imitate,
with whoops and hollers of anti-social hate,
sticking the High Street to the political stage
with an ancient and evil-smelling glue.
Be a card-carrying member of the human race
and kick the New Labour liar in the face,
for all those shabby ghosts haunting the ruins of this place
know now that their revolution vanished without a trace.
So we must hold our sides and laugh
at those "above good and evil" who went to Titipu
and Orphan Island in the sixties seeking relief
but only added to their dosage and self-pitying grief.
Now I see giants at the end of time
walking through a burning town

while massive beams bounce down
amid a galaxy of sparks, and the beasts
howl for entry at the gate, but too late,
for the last humans have opened the door
on midnight's hopeless chime,
and slipped through into their new estate
to become our ancestors-evermore.

Toffs Rule Rotten

It is a well-known fact that strap-ons are much debated
in the hallowed Upper House. For Lord Elgin brought back
an antique box from Athens which the Pasha swore dated
to the times of saucy Aristophanes, and in this cist
were ivory theatrical phalli which he donated
against the day when Ladies might adorn the red leather
benches.
But not until the degenerate days of the Female Eunuch's
mock-ups
were these prosthetics issued to the extended phallocracy
so that all might be equal wankers in that House of Cock-Ups:
thus today some disgraced aristocratic thief may be fated
to wear a phallus on his grey head, not for failing any test
but for being found out among the nation's best.

Sarabandha

Zeus in a vengeful mood once put shadows
into a box made of echoes,
and gave it to Pandora, saying :
"Little big-eyed lady, take this box of chocs,
but resist your urge to snack your fill,
and sit cross-legged on your red
lotus cushion, meditating, as a test of will."
Spotty Pandora was totally incurious,
despite the legends, but chewed bubble-gum,
sucked on jelly-babies and stole Mars bars
from corner-shops, which made her surrogate mum furious.
So, in due course, she found her belly rumbling
like a Blackpool tram at the thought of spam to cram,
or pickled onions, pork pies, or eggs and ham,
and her resolve went tumbling
and her palms grew sweaty at the thought
of the chocs in her box on her knee.
The vile shadows within tensed instantly
when the lid was lifted, but Pandora stabbed
blindly inside, hunger making her distraught,
and without a distracting fumble, grabbed
the first on top, slamming shut the fancy box.
The trapped shadow howled with rage
and then froze into a strange but palpable shape
when the magical girl made by smart Hephaestus
fixed him with a glance like glue upon the page
of living consciousness. "What's this ?" she scowled,
and the first shadow of mankind's ills, the Plague or Small
Pox,

was at once shrunk into something still foul,
but resistible, like all our fears and bogies,
when she answered her own question :" Stogies !
That old cheat has given me the wrong box!
Where's a match !" And she coughed and spluttered
as she inhaled the dread power of a really nasty trick
turned into a cheap cigar. All the shadows were thus reduced
into harmless ashes and Pandora lost weight, but was often
sick
a lot, until, years later, slim, pale and dark-eyed, push came
to shove,
and, stubbing out her last stogie in a hotel spitoon, she was at
last seduced
by a handsome youth, and gave up the habit for love.
Oh, by the way, at the bottom of the empty box, she found
a manufacturer's slip with numbers at an Italic slope,
and a legend : " PACKED FOR YOU WITH LOVE BY
HOPE"

The National Day of Vulgarity

-The twelfth of Solaire has been declared
a National Day of Vulgarity by Hyperion,
President of the Titanic Republic,
to commemorate the Treaty of Hyperstasis,
and Hera, Friend of the People of Titania,
has graciously accepted the Order of Prometheus
for her tireless peace efforts.
The Republican Daily
(14 Germinale 12008)
Hera was also commanded to produce a new work,
for performance in the Isometricon, that sacred cave
where was staged the huge success of her first play,
and when she asked my advice, I suggested she try an opera.
We sat in the TGWU works canteen by the entrance to Irem,
which was both a club and an assembly point.
Resting her ivory chin on her slim right hand,
in her left the long cheroot termed by the gremlins a spliff or
joint,
she remarked : "That would be a challenge to shirk,
as the only Titans with singing experience
are the Sirens." The idle gremlins fell about
with uncontrolled laughter until I broke in :
"Tartarus is changing fast, because Pan overdid the time
differential again, and they have a new generation
growing up with less hunting skills and more ambition."
I had to shout :"After the Peace, Silenus moved there,
as Master of the old Republic's Music,
and taught the accordion and balalaika without stop,
and became respected, sober, and did not touch a drop."

"Which is to say -what?" and a little frown revealed her as a
critic.
She looked like Maureen O'Hara in a frontier lair
with her checked shirt and the deerskin
breeches and fringed jacket which were part
of the Titanic national dress she was now so proud to wear.
On her famed red locks sat a stetson
with aepyornis feathers held in the hatband by a silver pin,
and about her waist like Aphrodite's magic girdle
fitted a leather belt with silver and jade, decorated
with great art by the hands of Titanic grannies.
"Which is to say that many of the most recent
generation have vocal chords like earthbound mortals,
and the ancient dialect of grunts and whistles, indecent
gestures and pulled faces is becoming
a dead language, used only in religious services,
like Latin in conservative parts of Europe."
I gave them all an encouraging smile, and, pausing at a wall-
socket,
I produced a casette player from my back-pack pocket:
"I recorded this to start you off - so listen, please."
The sounds of lovemaking filled the space,
for I had run together the tracks of some triple X DVDs
purchased from the Chinese slave workers, I fear,
to create a strange and menacing chorus of grunts,
which resembled the language of a long-lost race :
"sniff OOBA HOO OH GRUGGA BAG cough scream"
and so on et cetera. I thought it was a brilliant idea.
The gremlins fell about, holding their sides unable to speak,
Hera's maidens, Calypso, Circe, and all that feckless team,
giggled and turned red, Hephaestus said I had a cheek,
but Hera, as goddess of the marriage bed, nodded

thoughtfully, and asked : "But what about the operatic theme
?"
"Aha! "I replied : "Obviously a tale of change from old to
new,
a story of some rustic simpleton from the sticks,
arriving in Hyperstasis to learn new tricks.
A moral chorale, wherein the stoic country people defeat
the crafty ploys of urban twisters and so avoid Queer Street."
Before the Queen of Heaven could reply, there was the sound
of an air-raid siren, which raised us to our feet,
and from the air materialised a globe of glowing energy,
and two voices, one male, one female began to speak,
the man in New High Titanic, and the woman in Homeric
Greek :
(while round the globe ran subtitled English for my benefit)
"Comrades !
The United Action Council of the Central Committee
of the Revolutionary Socialist Party has been compelled
by the activities of manifold traitors to declare
a State of Emergency ! So that rumours may be dispelled,
Comrade General Prometheus, a flame in this time of despair,
will address the nation in ten minutes time.
Long live the People's Republic ! Let the People rule for
eternity !"
The globe faded. Martial music filled the air.
We stared at each other aghast, as muttering gremlins filed
into the room, took every available stool and chair,
or stood crowded around the rough-hewn walls.
Among them I noted a scattering of goblins, kobolds and
barrow-wights,
pale shokolotse newly arrived from the Cape,
all members of the TGWU, but no trolls who smell and eat

people,
get drunk on export apple-cider, start irrational fights,
then get arrested on the High Street and try to escape.
Finally the globe lighted again and the hologram it projected there
was of a young, handsome Titan with a black beard, and long hair
held in check by the traditional beret with the red star of freedom :
it was Comrade General Prometheus himself, and we all cheered,
myself included, for I had been honoured after the Great Inspiring Trek
on Chingford Hatch with the Brass Gong of the Company
of Promethean Firestarters, which I was currently wearing around my neck.
"Comrades ! In the name of the Provisional Government
in Presbai Purgos, the traitor Hyperion has been arrested
by partisans loyal to the Revolution and exiled to the Socialist
Autonomous Region of Equatoria , after his crimes were properly attested,
where he will renew his acquaintance with the rural masses of our nation,
and undergo a period of political re-education."
Prometheus, the idolized Hero of the Caucasus,
paused, and appeared to gaze searchingly around at us :
"Comrades, our ex-President was planning to use the clause
in the Treaty of Hyperstasis which allows the return
of all exiles to our old home, to raise an army and invade the sacred soil
of Mother Earth as fascist conquerors and foreign interventionists !

Amid cries of outrage, he added :" He would have made himself
a second Zeus ! In the presidential palace, we found outrages against our laws -
a royal crown, newly made in Paris by Cartier, and sketches
for a golden throne. For such treachery, he must now burn
beneath an unforgiving sun, chained to other ambitious wretches !"
"All this I can confirm !"came a deep and familiar voice,
and there stood mighty Herakles, ever the friend
of the Titans, a son of Zeus, but more a son of freedom,
now honoured as the Hero of the Atlas beside the Hero of the Caucasus,
wearing his famous lionskin hoody, freshly dry-cleaned.
After the cheering had died down, Herakles introduced
the new Comrade President of the People's Republic :
"Hyperstasis has fallen without a blow being dealt,
and a new leader has been produced from the many
to stand straight and proud where others have knelt,
a daughter of the wild woods and places uncanny,
who has put aside her pointed hat for a forage cap,
blown out her candles, packed away her crystals,
and assigned her cauldron for the guerilla's stew."
A beautiful young woman in the high-collared khaki tunic
of the People's Liberation Army with the three gold stars
of a general on her shoulders, stepped forward into view.
On her left arm was a red armband with two runic
sigils in the revised script on it : RED GUARD, that much I knew.
I did not recognise her. The Titans reflected as many human kin
as one found on a busy street in Stratford, Hackney, or even

Crewe,
and she, with her straight black hair and sepia skin
recalled old photos of native Americans. Hera gasped :
"It's Hecate ! "
The Goddess of Three Ways began to talk,
giving the clenched fist salute, which we returned :
" Comrades ! We must all work together to save our world,
and be ever vigilant to safeguard the freedoms
paid for in our blood in this long dispute against tyranny.
Be on your guard against traitors and Olympian spies !
Beware the running dogs of Zeus in sheepskin disguise,
those who pretend to love the people, but whose words are
hollow,
bankers and wankers, bossers and tossers,
sheep-shaggers, tail-waggers, Oxford debaggers,
husband-naggers posing as cocktail-party blaggers ;
gentleman's outfitters for tweedy bullshitters,
wife-beaters and cheaters who love to wallow
in the money-pit and honey-pit, reckless royals with the jitters,
goose-bummers, catchy tune hummers, kipper tie slummers,
sad rhymers and sadder mummers with down-to- the- last
crumbers,
short-order chefs and mail-order crooks all cooking the books,
in cahoots with bank-tellers and arm-pit smellers -
what a picture of greed and corruption they paint ! -
TV evangelists with open flies, demanding sexual restraint
from a cross-dressing suburbanite lover with a figure like
dynamite,
labour leaders with imperialist dreams, each a hyaena who
follows
phantasists and liars with jerky tongues and twitchy eyes,
car-jackers and bad meat packers, big heat packers,

human misery flesh-snackers, car-window blackers,
hackers and safe-crackers flooding out of Perivale
for the Titanic Special Sale and then pissing off back to jail;
entrepreneurs with the long tongues of curs,
and Pink-coated frauds, accountants with cruel spurs,
pandering to that dribbling crew of ever with us country-house
aristos,
middle-class lawyers and chinless haw-haw-hawkers, all
those in the throes
of the money-grubbing, scratch-card rubbing, cigar-stubbing
virus
of consumer capitalism, whom Hyperion would have called
in to buy us,
the peddlers of organised religion, the muddlers and meddlers,
the peddlers of medlars, fat men with claws chained to dogs
with huge paws,
investment bandits, golf club rejects and stock market outlaws,
all raiding our stores, ringing our bells and banging on our
doors,
like a plague of Thatchers and mad grinning Blairs spat out by
a dying world,
a place where snobs need only open their gobs to get good
jobs,
and honest workers are treated as slobs, whom the rich bastard
robs !
Comrades, stick together, and we'll dustbin these fuck-faced
fakes!
Our great land of the endless plains and soaring white
mountains
breeds heroes galore from shore to shore, and dragons to soar
high o'er the shining rivers and reed-guarded lakes,
and will be a model for all those born of Gaea, whether

stick-in-the-mud earthbounders or our own proud pioneers. !"
We all shouted :"Long live the People's Republic !"and gave three cheers,
sang (of course)"The Bonnie Blue Flag"and the "Song of the Steppes":
"Land of the birch tree and the endlessly undulating meadow,
all thy sons and daughters will heroically fight and toil!
Let the sunflowers grow o'er the graves of foreign interventionists
and the war-torn Red Flag ever guard the Motherland's sacred soil !"
Hecate finally held up her long-fingered hand and then we all fell quiet,
as she announced an amnesty for political prisoners, condemned by Zeus,
now pardoned and freed by an emergency meeting of the Diet :
Ixion, who was to speed up the wheels of industry in a ministerial post,
Tantalus who was to raise wine production as Director of Agriculture,
and Sisyphus who would increase land reclamation by draining swamps,
and building new dykes along the equatorial coast.
There would be elections in a year, when she would campaign on a Revolutionary Five Year Plan, and women at last were given the vote.
As Hecate stepped away, though we shouted for her to come back again,
smiling, Rhea, Chair of the Women's Institute, plump and beaming, appeared :
"The Day of Popular Vulgarity (as renamed) will go ahead as

planned,
as part of an entire week of celebration, tea-dances, parades, cavalcades,
spitting contests, prizes for elongated pissing and shin-kicking with burning boots,
strip shows, hip shows, clip joints, hip joints with booty-bouncing boogaloos,
a Vulgar Boatman Singing Competition, and a new Celebrity Death March,
with dire personalities, swaggerers and snotty debutantes in shrinking shoes,
a Rowdy King and a Slutty Queen, a brand new Vandalisation Campaign
and adolescent cross-dressing, compulsory for some, even if distressing!
And because we now have revolutionary and popular views,
we'll also revive the Festival Hooligan of the Year Contest, with the Crude
Stomping and Traditional Fondling in the Nude, previously banned !
So keep on working at your costumes, because no effort will be in vain !"
All were thrilled and happy at the turn of events,
and it took a god to make the situation tense.
Out of a portal in the wall behind, stepped Set,
and at his side Silenus, in a new incarnation.
Both wore uniforms high in the collar, khaki tunic
above dark blue breeches tucked into fine leather boots.
Their caps had dark blue bands above the peaks,
and on their left shoulders were flashes : a white capital gamma :
which stood for the Grammatia or Secretariat of State.

About their waists were hung holsters for large calibre pistols.
Set stepped up and kissed me on both cheeks:" Sorry we're
late".
He gave me a hug and then stopped in fake surprise :
" What's this ?" He examined my gong, with hooded eyes:
"The brass gong ?" he sneered :" Quite a coup
for a has-been revisionist and outsider like you !
One who has difficulty in being part of the team !
I have the silver gong, and you haven't a prayer,
as I'm a proper Titan and a divine gent by birth,
and all envy my body, plus my lovely red hair,
and my medal's legit, not one issued by the ancien regime."
Then he rounded on Silenus :"Sergeant, arrest this reactionary.
The penalty for counter-revolutionary activities
is summary execution !" Silenus fumbled with his holster,
and as he drew the revolver, Diggit sprang on to the shoulders
of Sawmitt (always a sign that a gremlin meant business)
and cried :" Touch a hair of Uncle Mickey's head,
and I'll drill you !" He clutched a bronze drill from his tool-
kit,
and Sawmitt added : " And I'll clock you !" From his waist
he unwound the pendulum which had gone missing
from my grandfather clock a week ago - not surprising !
But frozen-faced Silenus squeezed the trigger as the leaden
weight
struck his arm, causing the bullet to fly upwards,
chip the corbelled ceiling and ricochet towards the front wall
narrowly missing Sawmitt's pet raccoon who was prising
gemstones from the priceless mosaic, make another turn
above the gaping mouths and shouts of exasperation,
and, to my horror, like some diabolical metal bumblebee
head directly at a spot right between my eyes.

Instead of a fold of Death's best black opera cape,
I saw instead a pale, freckled wrist covered in fine, reddish hair
as Hera snatched the missile from the air, so saving me
with one divine gesture from Set's malicious jape.
As angry gremlins and their pet raccoons raised hand and paw
to pin down the would-be assassins, then sat on them,
a fresh portal opened, and Hecate stepped through,
accompanied by the opening bars of "The Song of the Steppes":
"Ah !" she cried, "there they are ! Hold them fast, comrades !
We'll give these foreign interventionists a taste of the people's law !"
Now, Sawmitt's missus, Gringold was threading a needle
with bronze wire to sew up the Storm God's lips,
when I snatched her hand back :"That you musn't do !"
" But Uncle Mickey," protested the lovely mother of two,
"we can't allow him to place on us a dreadful curse!"
"Ah, the Icelandic sagas say that the dwarves did that to Loki,
and their hasty actions only made things worse,
bringing on the Twilight of the Gods in a final Reign of Hell,
and I opine that this tale was not a record, but a prophecy."
I went on :" Look at them. Both are under some alien spell."
For Set was muttering, beneath the gremlins:" What happened to me?"
and Silenus was holding his head in his hands, ashamed of facing the room.
Hera, holding up the bullet with the others taken from his gun,
agreed : "These are magic bullets, made of silver by the Jinn."
Thus began a long debate, during which Tokmat, the raccoon,
glided to my side and, with great delicacy, presented one
item from his swag. a beautiful tear-drop of precious amber

which I placed in my pocket, tickling him absently under the chin.

Hecate finally agreed to strip Set and Silenus of their citizenship,

declare them persona non grata, then with a bewitching grin, place them in my custody, on parole. So I took them in.

-The City Learns a Lesson from the Peasants *by Hera,*

originally billed as Farmer George in Town,

will go down down in our history not only as the first

opera to be composed in Titania, but as a masterpiece from the pen

of revolutionary art, depicting as it does the triumph

of the old values of the workers and peasants, such as honesty and hard work, over a bunch of conniving city con-men !

The parallels with our recent popular uprising against the accursed

Gang of Forty Thieves *are clear, with Hyperion cast as the Crooked Big Boss.*

Alas ! Poor Herakles missed out on the Festival Grand Hooligan

prize to Antaeus, released by amnesty from maximum security in Presbai Purgos.

Herakles was supreme in the Vandal's Circuit, the Cat-Call and Buffet,

the Shin-Kicking with Burning Boots, the Grab the Girl in Studded Stays,

and was way ahead in the Big Grope and Buttock Bang,

when his wife, Hebe, an Olympian who does not respect our ways,

grabbed the big boy by the ear and yanked him out of the Pentathlon Orgy Peculiar.

He was thus only awarded the silver medal as Hooligan

Superior,
and the bronze went to the freed political prisoner, Gaius
Caligula.
As usual Charon won the Vulgar Boatman Singing Competition,
making a meal of his "Fucking Boating Weather" *rendition,*
and all contestants in the Celebrity Death March died this
year,
giving rise to such delight that the entire city rocked from the
cheer.
The People's Daily (13 Solaire Year 0)

Stones Written Upon By Stars

Beneath my house lies hidden Irem, the lost City of Pillars
where the Lesser Jinn held their balls and distractions
for our ancestors, and sought out mortal mates,
giving rise to legends of Giants and their stalking Killers..
Here is the Great Library of Sothis, a main attraction,
with its half a million tablets of chalcedony plates, ·
translated by Thoth into his Corpus Hermeticum.
Here is the Lounge of Ighlam Baz, the burlesque prince,
where once Herakles sipped nectar through a straw
and observed the bump and grind with half a mind.
Here are the Temples of the Great Ones, Lord al-Debaran,
his adversary, Lord al-Ghul, and Beit al-Jauza, Sothis the
Wise,
Procyon and many others, all with their emblems,
sigils, flags and bright pennants for the benefit of the
earthbound,
for the Great Jinn recognise each other, not by words
or bits of painted cloth, but by their spectra,
and converse, not by sound, but by bursts of radiation.
And here Lilith set up court (by right of inheritance)
with her posse of very bad lovelies : Aphrodite,
Circe, Calypso, and others, though Bastet thought them
too juvenile and hung out with Hera and Mave.
No gremlins were allowed and a circular traffic sign
was stolen and modified to show a small green man
with a diagonal red line through him. It was later taken down
after Sawmitt, Diggit's cousin, took hammer and chisel when
pissed
and began to adorn the outer wall with dirty pictures,

all of a quality in the fine detail to arouse the envy
of a sculptor from Khajuraho, or that Swedish copyist.
This Sawmitt was a gremlin of parts, a vivid and cheeky rogue,
who sometimes wore a fishscale sark made from silver
sixpences to lead his raccoons and polecats
against the deadly wolverines and giant bandicoots
of the lower depths, following the Almagest and its helpful
routes.
This armoured shirt had latterly belonged
to his grand paternal ancestor, Scatterfrown the Proud, and
some said
(maliciously) that the old tyrant's mistress, Jilt, had been paid
in the silver coins by stripping boldly and unbethonged
in the Magpie's Merit donkey's years before,
when gremlins were gremlins, and did not deplore
such exploitation of the female form. (Today, of course,
both sexes work for equal pay and wear their green boiler-
suits
side by side, and many females don the supervisor's dungarees,
or the white coat of the metallurgist, as ready with a spanner
on a Saturday night as any horny-hand from Shift 10.)
Now the gremlins are a good-looking crew, both girls and
men,
each with a face and body of Praxitilene proportion,
and though the height of an eight year old child
look otherwise just like us. Green of skin,
in variant shades, all have black hair apart from one
in a hundred, when red hair sprouts from head to shin.
These redheads are deemed a veritable caution
by their peers and looked to for wondrous japes
and party tricks, quick wit to make you laugh a fit,
and are known to claim a bigger portion

of glory in the ongoing chapters of the Telchinomicon.
Of course, among these russet brows were Sawmitt and Diggit
ostentatiously numbered, and would you believe it ?
-of the fifteen workers in Shift 10, three had flaming hair.
And here I must point out that the Telchins cannot be seen
by humans over five years old, unless they are mad,
simple, alcoholic or very holy, or else poets of a certain sort.
Alfred Lord Tennyson pretended to see fairies, but saw nought,
Swinburne had long conversations with them after a bottle of
port,
but Larkin never saw a magical being of any kind all his life,
though he did see commies hiding under his bed, he did apply
himself to stopping black men from trying to steal his nude
photos of white women, and he spotted Jews everywhere,
thwarting him, but xenophobia is not an aid to opening the
third eye.
Now gremlins had built the lost city as payment to al-Debaran
for the secret of trans-dimensional engineering, way back then
before The Disaster, when they all lived on Mars,
which was due to be struck by a comet and rendered
uninhabitable. With the help of the Great God Pan
who installed a time-differential in our celestial corner,
they had the opportunity to convert Asphyx, the third moon
of planet Mars, into a huge transport for their nick-knacks,
and a number of Martian flora (like sunflowers and runner-
beans)
and fauna (like termites, aardvarks and horned vipers),
plus their vast libraries of knowledge in organic form
carried in the brains of marsupials. The parakeet,
by the way, is Martian by origin, and was once much more
intelligent, and used as a secretary bird, particularly
by older gremlins who needed to be poked awake

by a beak in the morning, or to be constantly reminded
about serious matters, like paying the coal bill.
"Pay up ! Pay up! Or freeze you old fool ! cawcaw caw !"
Their favourite working pet is the raccoon which has evolved
over time,
with a proper set of five fingers on each hand
to crack safes, and thumb a moist black nose at the law.
The raccoons, by the way, also had their pets (of a sort) :
the magpie and jackdaw to aid them in woderful sport.
The gremlins also are famous for having invented the windmill,
the music-hall, the can-can, conga and the original
"Knees Up, Mother Red" which was terraformed later.
They also created dodgem cars and canned beer,
bodices and basques, open-crotch knickers and top hats,
love-hotels, sin in the afternoon, French kissing, and Greek
love,
English mustard, Russian vodka and the Italian head waiter,
Belgian chocolate and Chinese burns, cheroots and music-hall
turns;
they invented nude playing cards, purely for strip-poker,
transvestism, S&M and pajama parties, French ticklers and
the feather boa.
But they are in no way responsible for doner kebabs,
call-centres, dress codes, shell-suits, the missionary position,
sauerkraut, winkle-picker shoes, night starvation
and all horrible things culinary, military or unmodish,
and they brought all their patents with them, as a precaution.
They had no currency of their own, and borrowed ours,
being good socialists, regarding capitalism as extortion.
Alas ! Some things were too vastly huge to lift
and abandoned lay the Great Martian Sphinx,
the Cydonian Pyramids and the graves of the early ancestors,

and most thought-provoking of all, the original volumes
of the Telchinomicon, stored in a huge cave, thirteen kilometres
below the cold surface of the red planet in hermetically sealed
rooms.
For themselves, they opened portals all over the earth
and walked through with a valise, or rode on camels
or llamas, both also native to the red planet.
But emptied of its treasures, Asphyx became unstable,
and fell into an irregular orbit. The gremlins stached
their heritage in caverns beneath the earth, taking ,when able,
a small sample of earth life with them to safety,
and so escaped destruction when Asphyx smashed
into the Yucatan and left the domicile of hapless dinosaurs
trashed.
Emerging, into a world of dwarfish mammals,
no longer a healthy Martian red in colour,
but now faded to a terran green for lack of sunlight,
they sighed, shrugged, and worked on problems of space and
time,
colonised the galaxy, and returning after a bit to consult the
texts
of their ancestors, found some hairless apes in reindeer capes
dealing each other (with relish) a nasty blow.
And the rest you know.

Stratford Wives

Stratford wives have tattoes on their arses,
and never shave their muscular legs :
or their hairy armpits and possessive female slits,
but they'll wrestle a pig in glistening mud for a bet
of just a quid or two, then go for a drink with the girls.
Riding 1,000 cc motorcycles three abreast
along the Broadway, each one a smouldering Titaness,
(usually followed by the Great God Pan on his Harley)
they hold up commuters for hours while traffic cops weep,
then peel-off like *Stukas* to bring commotion and burning
to West Ham where fat football machos sleep.
They shake their fists at the Valkyries in the skies
who, noses in the air, ignore their threats of violence,
then, grinding their teeth, try to find solace
In demolishing the Essex skin-heads in their pigsties.

Every seven years they sacrifice a husband
to the gods of the Underworld at a ghastly clam-bake,
and on their bitch seats are pretty boys at the wake,
flying the flag in drag, like sexual shape-shifters
sporting dubious tit-lifters of Taiwanese make.

There's no escape from a Stratford spouse
or her nagging mum with a droopy bum,
and they'll pursue a runaway hubby near and far
all the way to Reykyavik or Agadir, the louse !
His head will become a clubhouse trophy
And his testicles'll float in a jar,
and the Supreme Witch of Woolwich (for a joke)
will wear his tanned skin as a raincoat on the ferry's deck.
So take my word for it, O East End Men,

and eschew a night of ecstacy with such as these,
or you might find a ring on your finger,
that's as good as a noose around your neck.

The Margaret Thatcher Pyramidion and Necropolis

There's a certain Bulgarian, a child of wonder,
who used to be found in piss-soaked pants sleeping under
discarded sheets of corrugated plastic roofing,
and his people were old when Osiris was toothing,
when the Iraqi ziggurats were new,
and dragons flew like kites up there in the blue.
He's lived a hard life among brawlers and gutter-crawlers,
bare-knuckle maulers blowing crack smoke rings
in mushroom clouds out of their arses
whenever the cruising patrol car passes,
and he's witnessed a multitude of barely believable things,
port wine and blue-vein drinkers, wonderful willy-shrinkers,
shapes half-seen emerging from dusty crypts,
busted coffins, bloody winding sheets and midnight callers.
In his youth it was all prayer-mutterers and headbanging kneelers,
heavy breathers and under-achievers, rabbit slayers with golden retrievers,
versus mountain cutthroats and valley sheep stealers,
now it's all indistinguishable lumpen choking down pies in their sties
while the beaten toddler bleeds and dies.
He was lately waiting for the Games,
to tell fortunes for celebrities and no-names,
having lost his position as Titanic Master of Music,
and being deported for making bad political choices,
when Lilith gave him a job checking her invoices.
Her dad's old staff have no head for figures:

they couldn't add up or count - not for them the rigours
of double-entry book-keeping, but she saw in this sad old man
many hidden talents and a lack of self-esteem.
So she gave him a chance, asking him to devise a scam
to finance her plan, laying ten percent as agent on the table.
Of course she meant MEAT, that outer space treat,
the Mars Exploitation & Areological Trust : and he was able
in double quick time to come up with an extraordinary scheme
which was guaranteed to be an investment wet dream.
What's more, he demanded and got twenty percent for his fee.
Nervously, he showed me the plans of North Chingford rebuilt
inspired by a strange urban legend created by the Long March
of the Gremlins about a pyramid to hold Thatcher's mummy,
to be a memorial to her capitalist ideal of replacing milk with
a dummy,
of bolstering conspicuous consumption, and of transforming
bourgeois misery
into angst-free self-congratulation within a gated paradise:
the rewards of under-age tarts and cocaine created by free
enterprise
'specially for knowledge-stealing net-hackers, military
hardware shelf-packers, limo-jackers, men in bibs and nappies
gone stark raving crackers,
barons 'n Sharons, pluggers 'n muggers, treasure-seekers and
pleasure-wreakers
making them all by decree lovable, huggable entrepreneurs in
the city,
gigglers and girl-higglers, cruising continence-pants leakers
with bedroom eyes,
the cultural messengers of episcopal knicker-sniffing, drug-
squad snitching,
offering the wet T-shirt crowd a bewitching salvation from the

White Van Men.
who range from Perivale, (Gate to Peristan), as far as the
Essex we all despise,
that unknown country beyond the Black Stump and the Great
White Stone,
Essex, where they build houses of pine for East End swine,
land of onion-picklers and inside trouser-leg piss-tricklers,
stereotype shit-kickers in secret open-crotch knickers,
slog it out men who are big dog-fight bill stickers,
yet out with the kids can be sensitive bluebell pickers,
brutal race-horse nobblers and eel-gobblers, yet secret cock-
wobblers
in dark and dismal vandalised station toilets where a queer
can be made on any soccer special week-end to disappear…..
And the architectural concept of Silenus was a work of genius.
It was to be financed by the little old ladies of Chingford :
those baba-yagas who chew off their husband's face
while he lives, and dead keep his ashes on the sideboard,
old biddies who hate their families worse than the foreign
horde,
and make their wills to the benefit of the smug feline race.
A three hundred foot high obelisk, constructed of black basalt,
bearing bronze plaques with the names of subscribers -
£10,000 at the top, and half a million at the base-
was to be surmounted by a clear crystal pyramid
containing the sarcophagus with Herself and four disciples
under one lid.
A son et lumiere spectacular was in store, holograms
and projections on to clouds every midnight for all time,
bringing to life her Great Events, minor scrapes and poll-tax
crime:
starting with her famous snatching of the milk-bottle

from a five year old girl, and her gulping it down :
snarling "Gotcha !" with a sinister and intimidating frown.
Then, how she was shot out of a torpedo tube from a nuclear
sub,
a limpet mine between her teeth, to blow up the Belgrano tars ;
her great day of triumph in a purple cloak covered in palms
and stars,
face painted with raddle in honour of Mars, when Galtieri was
debagged,
then marched behind her chariot to Parliament Square to be
gutted,
his head cut off and coated in tar, set ablaze and catapulted
into the Thames like a flaming coconut, his emasculated torso
then dragged
by meat-hooks in the hands of ermine-clad lords to Westminster
Bridge,
and hung upside down for all loyal Englishmen to see;
how President Pinochet in his best Bat Man uniform did a
bungie-jump of glee,
dangling from a Royal Navy helicopter incontinently;
how she led the charge of the Metropolitan Police Seventh
Cavalry
against the striking miners, devastating town after town,
cutting off arms and heads with her sabre, blow upon blow;
how she paraglided across the Sahara to rescue her beleaguered
boy
from savage fuzzy-wuzzies, her darling who might have
carried through
a new imperial design for African slavery by one simple
surgical coup,
but was foiled by sinister Marxist forces; how she made a
citizen's arrest

of Arthur Scargill when he clutched a suitcase to his breast
supposedly crammed with two million dollars from the Libyan
Embassy;
but most of all, that historic act so beloved of the always
supportive press,
the baba yagas who ate the general, the White Van Men, the
Head Bobby,
and the junior ministers, who pelt each other with bread-rolls
in the lobby.
The Houses of Parliament are heated by horse-shit in great
piles,
brought in buckets by old retainers in top hats, capes and
toothless smiles
from Horse Guards Parade. This reliable and cheap fuel
powers the Victorian steam central heating for the Turkish
Baths
where MPs can relax with their rent-boys and tartlets cruel,
and is out of the reach of striking coal miners. Neil
had made a fawning speech of capitulation, rejecting King
Arthur
that day to distance himself from the Phoney Libyan Funding
Scandal,
and Queen Margaret was mortified by his escape from guilt
by association.
Grim faced, she had Norman and Geoffrey, two pillars of the
nation,
hold him against the Speaker's Chair while she opened his
trousers
and scooped hot, steaming horseshit down inside with the
Mace.
Little John hurled the excess dung upon each Opposition
bench,

as he would stale hamburgers to the homeless, ignoring the rotten stench.

Then, while poor Neil begged for mercy - but she was pitiless to his face -

Black Rod tied rope around his trouser bottoms to keep the stinking golden globes from spilling out. They retightened his belt,

and set him free to lament, so that he ran shrieking through the corridors:"I'm full of horse-shit ! Let eyes weep as the golden globes melt,

but save me from these demons of the Pit ! I'm oh-so full of horse-shit !"

Up rushed two Wardens of the Wainscoting, for so named are the Commons

Coppers, clad in velvet knee-breeches and tricorn hats, who drew

their swords and set about the Opposition benches, where MPs cowered

from the golden rain and lay on the floor, some (of course) begging for more.

All policemen love their Maggie, who had them showered with overtime and extra pay for their sacrifices in her civil war.

Poor Neil was trying to escape like a crippled stag with the wicked crew

of panting Tories on his heels, blowing hunting-horns in hullabaloo

and out for blood, and he was forced to seek false sanctuary from some bishops in the Lords who concealed him in the Titled Ladies' Loo.

- It was an event worthy of the reign of Charles I or James II, you see.

But he almost suffered the fate of Heliogabalus in the lavatory,
when those old men in wigs and purple frocks held him face-
down in the pan,
calling him an enemy of God and a propagandist of atheistic
despair,
all the while rubbing stinking horse-shit in his thinning hair.
For years after there was much sniggering talk
of how he made a pitiful piddle waddle of the Westminster
Walk,
pursued by two shrieking old queens in bedraggled purple
robes
picking up what fell from his pants, and pelting him with
golden globes.
• All this was witnessed by the Keeper of the Royal Shithouse,
I suppose,
an old man in tricorn hat and red gown embroidered with the
Tudor rose,
being the master of a trundling handcart bearing a gilded box,
who ran behind the trio crying :" My Lords ! The anarchist !
There he goes!"
-This portable commode has not been used since Frederick,
Prince of Wales,
was found dead on it, but still earns the Keeper twelve shillings
and fourpence
ha'penny every Maunday Monday, though now bereft of sales
of the noblest dung in the Kingdom, he is forced to beg through
the iron fence.
-For once men bought a turd for twopence farthing as an anti-
baldness rub,
and blushing ladies sought such as food for a special rose or
stunted shrub.
Alas, the Keeper of the Royal Shithouse can no longer wank

you off for a shilling, nor suck you through the railings, as too many Lords have of late
used their prerogative of free service in this regard from an Officer of State.
Not to worry ! Neil was later appointed Emperor in Brussels, and invented New Labour for men with moustaches who like men with muscles.
All his relatives got clever jobs, being made European nobs (though transitory).
Some even said that the Council of Europe had promised at his demise
to make of him a god by their decree and install him in the skies
as a minor star in the tail of winged Pegasus, with all his clan in tow,
but no almanac gives up a suitable sun, though the Almagest's pages show
that the al-Moravids named a deadbeat star and its gas giants : Darat al-Jahash,
translated into Spanish in the great library of Toledo as Culo del Cavallo.
Silenus then showed me the plans for the bronze statuary.
to be established in the square beneath the eternal stache
of the obelisk, held up like a finger signalling class victory.
There was to be a mighty, seated Maggie of shining bronze, clad in her tank commander outfit with goggles and combat bric-a-brackery,
her left hand clasping a huge union jack, her right outstretched flat
and bearing all the tiara-laden and uniform glittering Windsors gazing up at her in wonder like some debased and disgraced XXIst dynsty adoring Set's shadow on earth's shitty door-mat.

Every hour at a quarter past, a clepsydra gurgles rug-a-jug-jug-drug,

and a hidden organ plays :"It's that man again !" off-key a bit, and bent,

while up from the steaming bowels of hell rises a Blair all winning smiles,

the fingers of his right hand five Trident submarine cruise missiles,

in his left hand the flag which flew over Richard's disembowelment

of the Muslim prisoners at Acre, the emblem on the shoulders of the England Abteilung, the flag of the White Van Men and their cows,

that rag carried by illiterate lumpen with swastika tattoos on their brows,

while a self-satisfied voice (with conviction) pronounces from somewhere :

"TONIGHT THE LABOUR PARTY STANDS IN AWE OF TONY BLAIR !"

At these words, the missiles launch, red, white and blue like airshow smoking,

and Blair's forehead opens allowing a little gallows to rise out, from which dangles a sad figure wrapped in an Iraqi flag, choking and croaking.

But Margaret has no need of worshippers outside the pale, she rises from her throne, turns her back, and a sheet of flame from her tail

whooshes down upon this grinning simulacrum of a human being,

over this fag end, this swine so bereft of common shame,

who murdered over a million helpless Arabs, mostly women and children,

many of them sick babies denied medicines from the West,
this monster, here immortalised with a diabolical fame,
like some jackal Sejanus, serving a transatlantic Tiberius, and
then
he sinks back with the wail of the damned to the depths unblest:
"I'll be back !"comes a fading rail against adverse destiny's
harshest test,
"Albion needs me ! I'll see this wicked history is properly
rewrit !
I can solve all the problems of the Middle East with my
outstanding wit,
and reconcile the three Abrahamic faiths with application of
incisive shit !"
Then, in a distant, irritating whine : "You can't do this to me -
I won the Class War with my wisdom, my healing presence
and sincerity !
My portrait hangs on the wall of every council-flat and
maisonette,
suburban women worship me like a plaster saint or teacher's
pet.
I'm the best of Thatcher's children- I won't go down into this
final Pit !"
Two claw-like hands clutch at the rim of this infernal drain-
hole,
but from the surrounding sculptural tableau emerges a pair of
heroes :
Robin Cook stamps on his fingers and George Galloway
forces down the lid,
and, raving still, down the simulacrum of a human being
shrieking goes:
"You traitors and success-haters can't keep me off the lecture
circuit !"

I was speechless, but said at last : " Albert Speer could have learned,
I fear, so much from you ! Silenus, you have a gift for this !"
He pointed out the Necropolis behind its gates of cast iron,
and the inscription over it in all the tongues of Europe,
with at the top : GELD MACHT UNSTERBLICH.
Within were to be the sepultures of the rich,
marble statues of ennobled fishmongers and ducal bastardry,
wondrous sculptures of naked boy angels, gilded and smirking,
bearing aloft the emblazons, shields and trade tools of the dead :
for a used car salesman, a steering wheel of 10 % solid gold,
for the police vice-squad chief in the shadows lurking,
boy and girl angels handcuffed together, naked in the cold;
a marble statue of the Pompeian Sausage Master sticks a stupendous dick
on to the scale-pan to balance a great pile of swollen tasties;
and the queen of the supermarket chain displays a sculpture of dubious pastries
piled in a golden trolley, a cornucopia with processed horrors in aspic.
I covered my eyes and groaned : "What have you done?"
But Sllenus nudged me to open them and hear the fun :
" The money is paid, the deeds are presented, the land is ours,
but it need now never be built, those sphinxes, pylons and soaring towers.
For we've pulled a gigantic con, and long live Lilith, the Queen of Mars!"
"Then you've cheated the cheaters and legalised thieves, fixers of crashed cars,
purveyors of inedible crap mixed up in a witch's kettle from sugar and lard,

brokers and percentage-stokers, spam-crammers and ring-fence rammers,
all those Thatcherite strivers who'd buy eternity for as little as poss,
those who profit from the fate of the poor, and fear only a dread red loss !
My dear Silenus, you've applied to the bastards their own morality,
stripping them of their extorted profits, in return for a pauper's grave,
the life unmarked by statue or unearned memorial in the draughty nave."
"Treasures earn the envy of princes," he replied, "and the hate of the dispossessed, who beg for scraps at the rich man's gate.
As one driven by kicks and dogs from that selective portal,
I know that only the desire for revenge can be termed immortal."
Silenus paused, and went on :" The Telchins will transport
the Devil's daughter and her statue to Cydonia, never fear,
and help her found a colony, or at least have a holiday home to plan,
for they know she'll never give the humans leave to land,
and Mars will remain their sacred archive with her as unwitting guardian.
There will be no gigglers and higglers, pluggers and muggers, barons and Sharons, treasure seekers and base pleasure-leakers,
to sully the red planet like a mucky pup in a palace cup."
"But what'll they do with all that money? They don't give a fart
for profiteering .Will they buy their pets gold bowls inscribed RACCOON ?"

"The Telchins have no need of money. They'll buy a few works of art,

and use the rest to teach the warmongers to sing a different tune."

"And you ? Will you go with Lilith ?" I shook his arm to make him speak.

Silenus gave the smile of a little child receiving a birthday gift:

" I am going to Maha Meru to sit among the snows,

This pilgrimage is mine, for I have forsaken my old foolish life

of unending riot and morbid fun, and my last journey has begun."

A great heaviness settled down on my heart, as Silenus left my door,

and waving, was firstly a silhouette against the setting sun,

and latterly a shadow among many others, and I felt a knife in my heart

as I had felt it before, in the hand of a woman, and I fell upon my floor.

Thug

Beating up his wife
his shirt rose and his pants fell
exposing his arse.

Trickle Down Economics Haiku

The rich piss with grins
down upon the poor, giggling
to see it trickle.

Missing the Bus

Because of her tears
she could not see it and failed
to put out her hand.

Witness Haiku

Sir slippered just her
in front of 5C, but he
never chastised me.

DJET

Djet: Eternity -
all around the stone remain
only some fragments.

Mr Jocular and Mr Jugular are One Entity

There'll be an exorcism on the first of May,
and it'll last at least one whole day.
The Ilford Commercial Traveller will run
a blow by blow account for fun.
As an emissary of the end,
I wear metal flanges on my heels,
so that I can strike sparks
when I pick up fag-ends in the cemetery.
I can look into the earth and see coins
of the Almoravids, gold *solidi* of Constantinople,
and the bones of Viking warlords among the runs
of mole and badger.

From my unwashed hands can come a blessing
which any priest would die for, and often do :
but this acknowledgement of someone else's destiny
is simply not for me.
So, I'll duck out of the ceremony,
and sit by myself (one of my selves)
in a corner of the *Green Man,* drinking
something sickly, and pretend to be thinking.

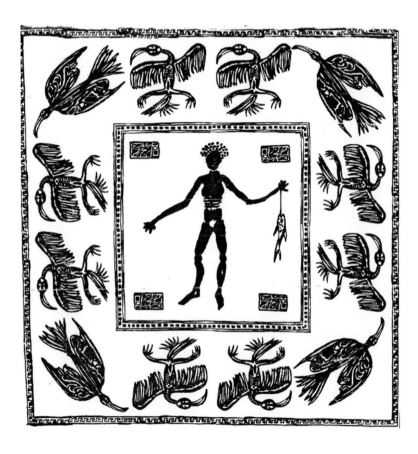

Acid Rain May Fall

Do not wear a leather coat today,
because the wind is from the north
and acid rain may fall.

Do not use the underground today
because the signals are busted on three lines
from the incessant acid rain on the old wiring.

When I see your cute face staring from the bus
I know you are not searching for me
and my tears are not salty, but acid.

Do not eat your sandwiches in the park,
for the pigeons have taken cover
and acid rain may fall.

Red Red Santa

A suburban Santa missed his step on an icy trail
and fell down the Wookey Hole, breaking his neck.
The foxes opened him up for Xmas dinner
while not entirely dead-
and the voles made nests in his boots.
Then one day in spring an *orang-utan*
escaped from a private zoo in Minehead
and, finding a red cap among the burgeoning shoots,
put it on his head and went to scrounge
on a long trip which ended in Walthamstow market.
Here, he was adopted by the local down-and-outs,
the alcoholics and red-nosed stumblers who lurch and lounge
among the crowds of sour-faced elderly shoppers
and was named as their Upright Man - Red Red Santa.

Santa came out on nights of the full moon
And bared his arse to the stars with a scowl,
like a carrion-eating baboon and not a wiser ape,
and was clever enough to wear a mask
under his hoody cowl. Howling like a wolf,
and shrieking like an outraged owl,
during our popular riots, three coppers
picked him up like a child's toy
to throw him through the window
of a struggling neighbourhood store,
but he knocked them senseless to the floor,
and drummed his chest with fiendish joy.

I was seated on a bench by the War Memorial
on Harrow Green, being entertained by Harry the Hobble,
the one-man band, Silly Mary (drunk as usual), Cecil
the Brush, the ex-vacuum cleaner salesman, Malcolm Marvel,

and eight or nine others, all untitled, and bearing names
like Grubby, Smutty, Handy, all easily forgotten, grey,
indistinct,
and old, while Red Red Santa held out his hat for coins,
to every social outcaste and street head-banger,
when Malcolm suddenly proposed that Santa should be our
own MP:

"He's our Santa, the Santa of the Poor, a Consumerist Anomaly,
the Santa of the Dispossessed, and we can get him
reclassified as genetically human. I know all this shit
because I was once a researcher at a classified utility,
where they worked on isolating the poverty gene,
so that losers like us could be eradicated lickety-split."

He ran a campaign with sign language,
giving the finger to the party flunkies
-and you should have seen what he called the Education
Secretary, dropping his sans-culottes pants
and shaking his dick. He's not thick !

For it will take an ape in a Phrygian cap to cure the ills of
greed:
carousing in the snug, peeling bananas with his feet,
"Oh ! Look at him," the ladies cry "He *is* so very sweet !"

And so we elected him to Parliament, though they tried
their reactionary best to exclude him as inhuman-
though that never in the past prevented three
quarters of the House from taking their seats,
but we proved his DNA was hominid rather than simian
and that he was sentient though lacking vocal ability,
and still able to communicate his thoughts by BSL.
He shat on the Tories from a great height, having swung
from beam to beam, and bent the mace

about that snidey PM'.s neck. They tried to throw him out
for being a mute, but such discrimination against
those with disabilities resulted in marches in the streets.

Now, his gestures are translated by a secretary and published
in the *Spectator,* and the lords and bishops hate him
for still wearing the red cap of freedom,
and refusing to swear allegiance to their Queen.
He proposes instead a Republic where education is free
for all and sundry, where all can show
two fingers to the pro-fascist press, and where all can know
that a clever ape is smarter than any Tory MP.

Under the Jacaranda Tree at the End of Daze

Step outside the flow of consciousness,
ignore the pangs of hunger, the head-ache
and the dry throat, and become the flow,
the buzz of otherworldly astral glow.
Leave the soccer-sucking, mother-fucking buggers
to their knifery-wifery and domestic
witchery-bitchery behind the neat hedges :
or, better yet, send them all packing
to Hell with a bit of a smacking
if they try to tough it up when we rough 'em up
one last time in the summer time's decadent glow.

Every witch needs a knight-errant on the run,
and you've got me, you lucky bitch,
and I'll reflect on this under the jacaranda
(my very own leafy verandah)
until Shaggy Doggy runs up and licks my face
one last time, before leaping up to swallow the sun.

Trolls in the Underpass

Have a hot dream night with nice wrestling
and more strippers than rippers,
like the monsters in carpet slippers
holding a glass to the dividing wall :
but always watch out for the magpies
at the window with intelligent eyes,
part-watching the swallows
heading south through darkening skies
leaving cats disappointed –
and that's no surprise !

Oh! Where are the bangle-janglers
dangling new-fangled handbags
over their wash-faded *Wranglers,*
where but following the High Jive Dominatrix
about to sky-dive on a single fix
in the underpass twilight dream
where things are never more than they seem....

This is the teaching of the *Lab al-Lahoot*
the Wisdom of the Superworld
where alchemists of the soul
take a grimy gander
at the flare of never-to-be-born despair
felt by a semi-conscious salamander :
then do a double de-clutch on the leatherette
madam's shaven crutch
because voyeurism
has never hurt so much.

Living in a Cave

Forget the foot-shaggers and suit-draggers,
the ancient gong-hoggers and poop-scoop doggers,
the bang-haggers and lonely tongue-waggers
who all look daggers at girls in the *hijab*
on the grey streets of Romford,
and pretend you live in a cave on a cliff
along with the stone sarcophagus
of a mummy wearing a gold scarab,
he's no trouble at all – and let this be your Batcave.
Then a different view of those ugly Essex witches
in their itchy-kitschy crimplene britches
will enchant your mind and save your soul :-
let the wicked rot in a row, for their dribbling curses
will benumb few manikins with health parlour tans,
except their own lousy menfolk,
busy stealing knickers from washing-lines
and never paying the mounting parking fines
on their perpetually untaxed white vans.

Back in 1998, when it seemed so modern and up-to-date,
Kinky Winky, the whorecock warlock,
made a woman out of Big Macs and gave her massive jugs
so that she take all macho men for mugs,
stealing their wallets for drinking money
while all the time calling them *honey*...
But she ran away (clever girl) from this new Pygmalion
and lives in the red cliff wall just along the way from you,
with some vengeful Harpies, flaked-out Bacchantes,
and many other refugees from pig-sty Becontrees.
Maybe you can all get together
and stick a switchblade into those white van tyres
making sure that these future captains of industry
won't get as far
as even Kinky Winky in his gettaway car ?

Totemic Hoppity

Working wasters love chocolate sundaes
and vote for lots and lots more,
though its production keeps the producers poor,
Theme Park billionaires love Family Fun Days
and put fliers through your door
to entice you to a honkey-tonk donkey bonk
(in your own mind) like a blubber scrubber
with a custard pie on her raddled thigh.
A wasted life spent staring,
not one spent *seeing*,
full of the gasping of the drunk
in the dark shop doorway peeing.
But everybody overspends
to achieve their self-gratifying ends
without a thought to the mounting debts.
The geek in the WC
has locked the door against discovery
but his debt-collector is still hiding
in the litter-covered shrubbery ;
the local lads sit in a car
outside his flat in the evening gloom
waiting for the light to go on in his room –
they wear grey coarse weave denims
and black leather *Gucci* boots
for their jabber-wobble blood-bubble trouble
prior to their delivery of the grief-giver
to the waters of the unforgiving river.
Such men are frequently born of soapsuds and spite
rather than fire and passion, and like to spend
their secvr5et quality time at night
letching over the photos of past victims,
arranging and re-arranging them by hair, height,

sex or type of shoe, reclassifying without end....

Anchises wails on the banks of the Styx
and that once lovely Hermione
finds the darkness does not set her free
when she bends over the bloody offering
and licks and licks...

A Thoughtful Gesture

The boss made his hide
into continence panties
for his dear old dad.

Not in Costume

Not in costume move
the gigglers and higglers
and I do not approve
their energising oranges
with nude cool drool
like little kids from school.
The paedos with dingle-dangle *credos*
like to snap them in the pool,
and have summer passes to all the lidos,
and open-fly peepers, washing-line creepers,
get hot and itchy
at the view (*wouldn't you, too*)
of tight frocks and stocking shocks
letting down the tires
of cars with plates from the shires:
summer is a spanner
in the tool-box of revolution
and the bum-paddling underwater
climax bungler will find no solution
to his anxiety in the sun.

Greed is A Right of Birth

Self-obliging little twerps
who pull the trigger
like wannabe Wyatt Earps
are excluded for no right of birth,
snigger, snigger, snigger …
So look for a snooty beauty,
meddling in arse peddling
and a high hat atop each Tory brat –
for I've never thought that that
could disoblige a compulsive submissive
in sock-suspenders hanging from a beam
in a Belgravia flat.
Our masters go on benders
with all the genders
when their stocks go up and soar
and really enjoy
watching their police lackeys
kick the shit out of a working-class boy:
for that's the way it's always been,
in this land of beggars at the rich man's door.
All the prophetic libel
you find in the Bible
cannot cut their compassion deficit
down to size, so let them pray, pray, pray,
and read sermons of thrift,
because greed is no common gift,
and donkeys have to bray, bray bray.

With the Sound of Fiddles along the Shore

While the City bogey men hoot and hum :
"Let the markets come !",
the shooters and looters
stood up against the wall
suffer a truly catastrophic fall :
and the politicians with their libraries
of books with fascinating, gold-leaf spines
try to pen some memorable lines
about our interesting times,
and big-boobed chicks
with monstrous strap-on pricks
storm around their Belgravia pads
urging them on to realize their crimes –
amid this monstrous glimpse of doom
the ghost of William Blake,
that sad old flake,
rings his pale, ink-stained hands
and whispers on the wind : "Albion ! O Albion!"
But none of the weepers and creepers,
the shakers and takers, the fox-hunt leapers,
the mistresses of noisome slums
who apply hazel switches to our masters' bums,
not even the grinning cop with oustretched palm
can envisage any return to the traditional calm
or ignore the Writing on the Wall :
THEFT IS GOOD – feel it and steal it !
Remember that in the shopping mall.

Yet More Bad Poets

Paul Verlaine was always a pain
and Philip Larkin liked to watch girls
again and again
clad in studded leather togs
fight on stage like sex-crazed dogs-
and, as for that Wordsworth dope
he loved only his sister – what a hope !
T.S. Eliot was a Yankee twat
dolled up like an English aristocrat,
and what is worse,
based all his dribblings
on mistranslations of Chinese verse.
Shelley, I must say, was a wonder,
and Keats could be good,
but Byron, always misunderstood,
gave up a life of potatoes and gravy
to found the Royal Hellenic Navy.
Real Englishmen cannot write a jot
unless it's about that Froggy Lancelot,
and even Dai Thomas in his cups,
tried too much to please –
and lost the plot.

Buzzword Lightning Strike of the Entitled Drapers

Every tallyman and every ledger ckerk
shall burn a candle in the dark
to enhance the glories of the untaxable,
extempore and expatriate Tories
who love to spread precognitive stories
about the unentitled young.
His Lordship will only turn up for a handout
or a comradely bung,
to have his tweeds stuffed with used
fifty pound notes, but still feels a need
to hoard his guineas overseas
safe from the teenage communists
who prefer the Soft Shoe Shuffle
and the Wall Street Kerfuffle
to the black-tied Mansion House Splitz.

The Vampire Wife

Wanting a colder, dead
thing in her bed, she bit
her banker husband.

Penny Da

The East End is the home of strippers and rippers,
monsters in specs and carpet- slippers,
a place where the troll in the Underpass
will give you a filthy sign, and bare his arse:
Captain Dreck got a bolt in his neck
after a night out in Walthamstow,
all for making the wrong signals
to a man in a shabby raincoat,
and you must choose between going home
in a basket or going to Church in a casket
when you laugh on a falsetto note.

Hathor is a sad old cow and drinks like a fish,
and used to live in a run-down alley in Thebes-
or was it Holy Memphis ? Now she's got the DTs
and prophesies doom in the gloom on her knees.
My chum, Set the Desert Rat, hits all the high soirees
and the afternoon swinging affrays and he tells me
when to run, when to lift up a flap
in the goatskin tent of our sad Unreality
and leg it like mad when you hear the rap-rap-rap
of the Raven on the chamber door.
Let round-bottomed Hathor take a crap
in the unswept gutter, and carefully ignore
the onlookers in their dim living-rooms
plucking at the flowered drapes.

For in the real reality we seekers after truth
must imitate or innovate, sit with the rotten
moneychangers and be forgotten,
or pace on with a heart that beats
for Freedom, however threadbare her winter coat,
and seek blazing magic in mean little streets.

Unromantic Haiku

She snatched the carpet
from under my feet, but I
never fell for her.

Smack on the Cheek Haiku

Staring at her bum,
I tripped and fell down the stairs,
landing on my rear.

Fiddling Haiku

It was a riddle,
she'd give her tits a twiddle
playing her fiddle.

The Melting Mixture of my Consumerist Dreams

I see no Tunnel of Love into the hearts
of the Association of Cheap Police Officers,
except one for brain-takers and plane-makers,
train-shakers and pain-makers,
because bed-wetters end up go-getters,
successful flat-letters with Irish setters-
the sort of snobs who know their betters,
worshipping sex-cheaters and flight-meeters,
all turning into wife-beaters when their dunghill teeters,
because a nation of sheep-bleaters
can never turn Omegas into Zetas.
They'll end up against the wall without mercy,
listening for the sound of safeties off,
every would-be money man and minor toff,
while their masters decamp to some distant hell-hole
like the Isles of Man and Wight, or even Jersey.

FOREIGN WORDS IN THE TEXT

Achni devi (Romani) : the good goddess, Kali (whose name is not normally spoken)

Akhet (Egyptian) : the Inundation of the River Nile

Almagest (Arabic) : a guide, or atlas

Bain-Marie (French) : both a cooking and an alchemical utensil for gently heating substances or food, invented by Maria the Egyptian.

Conga (W. African) : a dance

Djet (Ancient Egyptian) : eternity

Dosh (Romani) : money (slang from dost "friend" or possibly dust "shit")

Hubris (Greek) : overbearing arrogance which invites divine retribution

Maskara Aballabat (Turkish) : a commotion in masks

Namaste (Hindi) : Gesture of hands with palms together in greeting or worship

Parth Lludd (Welsh) : The Gate of the Sun, as at Tiahuanaco.

Poteen : (Irish) illicit distilled liquor, moonshine (pronounced pocheen)

Qal qalbi (Arabic) : "my heart speaks"

RAMA TERI MAYA JALA BICHAYA (Hindi) : literally "Rama escaped thy Net of Illusion", part of a sacred song in honour of the god Rama

Sambhur (Hindi) a large deer

Sekhetu A'aru (Egyptian) : The Blessed Fields, Heaven

Telchins (Greek telhini) : mischievous elves employed by Hephaestus, gremlins.

Greek names are represented in the Latin spelling convention: Silenus not Silenos

Dionysus not Dionysos (and definitely not Bacchus)
Hephaestus not Hephaistos (and definitely not Vulcan)
Cerberus not Kerberos
etc

However, there are two exceptions : Eros, whose name is spelled the same in Latin and Greek, is once referred to as Cupid, and Herakles is always used instead of Heracles as an heroic exception, and as Hercules never.

In the same way, Odysseus is always used, and not Ulysses. Though in modern Greek this heroic name is pronounced Othisefs.

Sanskritik names related to the Hindu gods and places sacred to them, and words related to Buddhism, are rendered in a form of phonetic spelling widely adopted in general books on mythology to avoid the dots and dashes and acute accents used in more scholarly texts. Old imperial spellings from the days of the British Raj are avoided : thus, Vrndavan, not Brindaban.

Egyptian gods are usually referred to by their Greek names, such as Isis and not Wa'aset or Thoth, and not Djehuty, apart from Set who was known to the Greeks as Typhon.

PLACES MENTIONED IN THE TEXT

The Black Stump : this is the remains of an oak tree in Wanstead. This ancient tree was cut down during the M11 rebuilding. An act of official vandalism which I trust the Furies will punish !
The Great White Stone : this is a Roman mile-stone just off the A11 roundabout.
The Harrow Green War Memorial : this is an obelisk erected in honour of the dead
of the World Wars.
The Obelisk : this is a much larger obelisk in Chingford, which was erected to mark the Greenwich Meridian.

THE FIRST TRILOGY
GODS & DEVILS IN LEYTON
A WHIRLWIND IN LEYTONSTONE
LEYTON GREEN

THE SECOND TRILOGY
LEYTON UNDERGROUND
LEYLINES
HARROW GREEN

Would you like to see your manuscript become a book?

If you are interested in becoming a PublishAmerica author, please submit your manuscript for possible publication to us at:

acquisitions@publishamerica.com

You may also mail in your manuscript to:

**PublishAmerica
PO Box 151
Frederick, MD 21705**

We also offer free graphics for Children's Picture Books!

---

www.publishamerica.com

Lightning Source UK Ltd.
Milton Keynes UK
UKOW041950281212

204185UK00001B/15/P